Lost
AT Sea

BY

Ed Hanson

THE BARCLAY FAMILY ADVENTURES

Development and Production: Laurel Associates, Inc.
Cover and Interior Art: Black Eagle Productions

SADDLEBACK
PUBLISHING·INC.
Three Watson
Irvine, CA 92618-2767

Website: www.sdlback.com

ISBN 1-56254-555-8

Printed in the United States of America
08 07 06 05 04   9 8 7 6 5 4 3 2 1

CONTENTS

MEET THE BARCLAYS

Paul Barclay
A fun-loving father of three who takes his kids on his travels whenever he can.

Ann Barclay
The devoted mother who manages the homefront during Paul's many absences as an on-site construction engineer.

Jim Barclay
The eldest child, Jim is a talented athlete with his eye on a football scholarship at a major college.

Aaron Barclay
Three years younger than Jim, he's inquisitive, daring, and an absolute whiz in science class.

Pam Barclay
Adopted from Korea as a baby, Pam is a spunky middle-schooler who more than holds her own with her lively older brothers.

CHAPTER 1

The Invitation

Aaron sighed when he heard the phone ringing in the kitchen. He was in his room working on a science project. Since he was waiting for a call from his friend Brad, he headed down the hall toward the phone.

But his sister Pam speeded past him.

"I'll get it! It's probably for me, anyhow," she shouted as she grabbed the telephone.

"*Daddy!*" Aaron heard her scream with excitement.

"Hi, Buttons! How're you doing?" her father said.

"I'm fine, Daddy. Are you coming to visit us this weekend?"

Aaron went to the extension phone.

"Hi, Dad," he said.

"Aaron, my boy! What are you up to?"

"Schoolwork, Dad. Are you coming to see us soon?"

"Well, actually, guys, I was hoping that you'd come and visit *me*. I'm off work the last two weeks of July. How would you like to cruise the Bahamas with me on a 42-foot sailboat?"

Both Pam and Aaron jumped with excitement. Spending two weeks on a boat with their dad sounded great.

Both kids spoke at once. "That sounds terrific, Dad!"

"First, I've got to clear it with your mom. Tell her I'll call tonight to discuss it with her. And tell Jim about the trip, too," their father added.

"Oh, rats! Do we have to take *him*?" Pam asked jokingly.

"Yes, Buttons. I need Jim to help me run the boat. But don't worry. We'll have a job for you."

The minute Ann and Jim came home, the younger kids told them about the phone call from their father.

"He's going to call you tonight to talk it over. You *will* let us go, won't you, Mom?"

Ann Barclay thought about it for a minute. Then she said, "Well, I guess that'd be okay if you really want to go. How about you, Jim?"

"I'd sure like to go," Jim said. "But I have to be back by August second for the first day of football practice."

"Dad knows that," Aaron chimed in. "That's why he picked the last two weeks of July."

"All right, then, it's settled," Ann said. "I'll make arrangements with your father when he calls tonight. He's a good sailor, so I know you'll be safe."

That evening Paul Barclay called his ex-wife. Their conversation went on for almost an hour. Even though they were no longer married, there was still a strong affection between them.

Paul said he'd send three tickets for the flight to Miami. Then he urged Ann not to worry about the kids.

"I'll take good care of them!" he promised.

CHAPTER 2

Getting There

On July 14, Ann Barclay drove her three children to the airport. She hugged each of them and told them to have a great time. Then she said, "Be sure to give your father my love."

Aaron popped in, "Mom, if you still love Dad, why did you get a divorce?"

"We don't have time to discuss that now. Besides, it's none of your business," she said with a smile. "Now get out of here. And have fun!"

Paul was waiting at the Miami Airport. He waved as his three children got off the plane. Pam was the first to spot him. She ran up to him and jumped into his arms. *"Daddy!"*

Paul gave her a big hug.

"Hi, Buttons!" he whispered in her ear. Pam loved the nickname her father had given her when she was three.

Then Aaron and Jim hugged their dad.

Paul put his arms around all three of them and said, "This is going to be a *great* trip! We'll sail all over the Bahamas. We'll swim and snorkel and do some fishing. And, Jimbo—I hope you remember the sailing lessons I gave you. I'm going to need your help running a 42-foot boat."

"I remember, Dad!" Jim said.

"Okay. Let's claim your bags and get down to the boat."

The *Sea Mist* was moored at the far end of a long pier. The kids saw that the vessel was dark blue with white trim. She looked sleek and fast.

Pam looked up, up, and up. She couldn't believe how big the mast was.

"Gee, Daddy, look at that mast! It must be 100 feet high!" she exclaimed.

"Well, it's not *that* big, Buttons! But it's tall, all right," her father said. "Let's go on board and I'll show you around."

Standing on the stern, Paul pointed out the helm of the *Sea Mist*.

"This is where we steer the boat," he explained. "The large wheel controls the rudder. And those dials and gauges provide the helmsperson with important information."

Next, they went into a small room on the deck that Paul called the pilothouse.

"Our navigational equipment and marine radio are in here," he said.

The big table in the middle of the pilothouse was covered with charts that looked like maps of the ocean.

Space was limited down below. There were three small cabins where they would sleep. A small stove and refrigerator were in the galley. The kids were glad to see that the *head*, or bathroom, was complete with a shower.

"Jim, you and Pam put all the clothing and gear away," Paul said. "Aaron and I will go to the market and buy food for the trip. Does anyone want anything special?"

"Peanut butter!" Pam yelled. "Don't forget about the peanut butter."

"And frozen pizza," Aaron added.

"Don't you guys ever eat *good* food?" their father asked with a laugh.

"Only when Mom makes it," Jim laughed. "Those two would live on junk food if they could."

"Look who's talking!" Pam cried out with pretended anger. "You eat more ice cream than anyone I ever saw!"

"Forget it, guys. *I'll* pick the food," Paul said. "When you're hungry enough, you'll eat it. And I promise you're going to get hungry, because we're all going to be working hard."

Paul and Aaron headed off to the store while Jim and Pam started to put away their things.

At the store, Paul filled two carts with food. He expected to be at sea for 10 to 12 days—and there were four mouths to feed! Aaron added plenty of frozen pizzas, cookies, and candy bars.

Finally, his father said, "That's enough junk food, Aaron. It's a wonder your teeth haven't already rotted and fallen out!"

"Oh, gee, Dad, we're on vacation! You sound just like Mom now. And by the way—Mom sends you her love."

"That's nice," Paul said with a smile. "When you get home, be sure to give her my love, too."

Aaron didn't say anything. But he wondered why adults were so strange. If his mom and dad loved each other so much, why did they get divorced? He couldn't figure it out.

Back at the boat, they all pitched in to get the food stowed. When everything was put away, Paul checked his list one last time:

- Food—OK
- Fresh water—160 gallons
- Fuel—100 gallons (good for 400 miles)
- Fishing gear—OK
- Diving gear—OK
- Sleeping gear—OK
- Flashlight—check
- Radio and radar—check

"Is there anything I've forgotten?" Paul asked himself.

"Oh, yes—there's one final rule, kids," he said. "When you're on deck, *everyone* wears a life jacket. Got that? Okay, I think we're finally just about ready to get going tomorrow."

CHAPTER 3

The *Sea Mist*

At 6 o'clock the next morning, it was time to start the trip. After Jim cast off the bow and stern lines, the *Sea Mist* motored away from the dock. Paul was using the 25-horsepower engine until they were out in open water. Then he'd raise the sail.

Jim stood ready to raise the mainsail at his father's command. Before long he heard his father call out from the helm, "Take her up, Jimbo!"

It took all Jim's strength to crank the huge sail to the top of the mast. Then, as the wind filled the sail, the *Sea Mist* listed 10 degrees to starboard and Paul shut off the motor.

Now the only sounds were the wind and the splashing of seawater on the hull. It was quiet and peaceful.

Aaron and Pam were still asleep.

"Jimbo!" Paul shouted. "How about

getting me a cup of fresh coffee?"

Jim went down to the galley. He poured his father a cup of hot coffee and brought it up on deck.

"Thanks," his father said. "Now tell me how life's treating you, son."

"Not too bad, Dad," Jim answered.

"Are you still lifting weights?"

"Yeah. I'm trying to work out at least four or five days a week."

"What are you benching now, Jim?"

"My best lift so far is 185 pounds."

"That's great, Jimbo!" Paul said. "I couldn't come close to that when I was your age. Keep at it and it won't be long before you're lifting 300 pounds."

Then Pam interrupted their man-to-man conversation.

"Why didn't you wake me?" she asked as she came up on deck.

"I thought you wanted your beauty sleep, Buttons," her father answered with a smile.

"If that's the case, you'd better go back

to sleep, Pam," Jim laughed. "You aren't all that beautiful yet."

"Ha! Well, *you're* not all that handsome yourself," Pam giggled.

Paul chuckled. "If I have to listen to you two arguing, I'll drop you off at the first island we hit. This is supposed to be a peaceful trip."

The *Sea Mist* was doing about five knots. They'd been at sea for about two hours by now. The Florida coastline was barely visible.

Paul had set a course for Grand Bahamas Island, about 100 miles away. He figured they'd be there by the next morning. But you can never be certain when you're sailing. If the nice breeze dropped off, they'd arrive much later.

At 8:30, Paul was getting hungry.

"Hey, Buttons!" Paul yelled. "How about making us some breakfast?"

"Oh, Daddy," she said, "are you going to stick me with all the jobs *you* think are 'girl's work'?"

Paul quickly changed his mind. "My mistake, kiddo! You're absolutely right. I stand corrected. How about instead I teach you how to steer the boat. We'll get Jim and Aaron to make breakfast."

Pam took the wheel, and Paul showed her how to follow a compass course. Right now, there was no land visible in any direction—just water. Without a compass, Paul explained, they wouldn't know what direction they were going. The compass was the most important single piece of equipment for a ship at sea.

Before long, Paul saw that Pam was confident in her job.

"It's all yours now," he said. "I'm going below and see how breakfast is coming."

Pam felt a surge of pride. She was running the boat alone! No one else was even on deck. She wished her mother could see her now.

CHAPTER 4

Nights at Sea

When Paul walked into the little galley, Aaron and Jim both said, "Who's running the boat?"

"No problem. Your sister's got the helm," Paul answered.

"Gee, Dad, she's only nine years old! Do you think she can handle this big boat?" Aaron asked.

"Stop worrying, Aaron. She knows what's she's doing. By the end of this trip she'll be a great sailor," Paul answered.

The rest of the day was wonderful. Each of the Barclays took turns at the helm, steering the boat. The breeze stayed strong, and the *Sea Mist* plowed ahead at a steady five knots.

Every few hours, Paul went into the pilothouse. There, he checked their position and listened to the marine weather forecasts. Everything was going well.

Since they'd be sailing all night, it was necessary to set up a schedule for manning the helm. Aaron took control until 8 o'clock when Jim would relieve him. Then, after grabbing a few hours' sleep, Paul would take the wheel at midnight.

The night was beautiful! Countless stars sparkled overhead. Jim was almost sorry to go below, but he was tired, and he knew he needed some sleep.

Paul sailed all night. At daybreak, the *Sea Mist* rounded the western tip of Grand Bahamas Island. Within another hour or so, he anchored the boat in a protected cove. The crystal-clear water there was about 20 feet deep.

Minutes after arriving, everyone put on bathing suits. Soon they were enjoying the warm, tropical waters. Wearing their face masks and snorkels, Jim and Aaron began to explore the ocean bottom. Fish of all colors and sizes were everywhere!

Later that afternoon, they took a small, inflatable boat to the beach. Paul and Pam sat on the sand talking while Jim and Aaron explored the island. After a day and a half at sea, they felt great to be back on land again.

That evening after dinner, Paul asked what everyone wanted to do the next day.

"We have no schedule," he said.

"I like it right here," Aaron said. "I wouldn't mind staying here another day."

Jim and Pam quickly agreed. So the family spent another day swimming and snorkeling in the cove.

After supper on the second evening, they pulled up anchor and set sail for Little Abaco Island. They would sail all night. If the breeze held up, they'd be in the lee of Little Abaco by midmorning.

Paul and Aaron took the helm. Jim planned to relieve them at 1 o'clock. But at 10, Aaron nudged his father.

"Dad, what's that red light off the port bow?" he asked.

Paul turned and looked. Sure enough, off on the horizon, he could see a red light glowing in the darkness.

"That's the portside running light of another vessel, Aaron. We'd see a green light if we were looking at his starboard side. All ships at sea have these lights. They let other vessels know which direction you're going. And that helps sailors to avoid collisions."

"I don't see any lights like that on our boat," Aaron said.

Paul smiled. "That's because you haven't looked hard enough, son. Look up toward the top of the mast."

Aaron looked up. Near the top of the mast, he saw a green light on the right and a red one on the left.

"Why are they up so high, Dad?"

"Because they're easier to see the higher up they are," his father answered.

Aaron looked a little puzzled.

"You're forgetting an important fact about the Earth, Aaron," Paul continued.

"What's that?"

"The Earth is round."

"Come on, Dad. I know that," Aaron said. "*Everyone* knows that!"

"Sure, Aaron. But remember that we see in a straight line."

Paul pointed ahead of them. "The Earth starts to curve about seven miles to the horizon. Anything farther than that is hard to see unless it's tall."

At 1 o'clock in the morning, Jim came up on deck. It was time to let his father and brother get some sleep. Paul explained the course he wanted Jim to follow.

Paul yawned. "Wake me if there's any problem," he added. "Otherwise I'll relieve you at 6 o'clock."

Now it was Jim's turn to enjoy the peaceful solitude of a night at sea. Alone on deck, his thoughts turned to home. He missed his mother and wondered how she was doing.

He also thought about football. Practice would be starting in about a week. He knew he'd make the team, but would he be a "starter"? The five hours went by quickly. Before Jim knew it, his father was back on deck.

"Morning, Jimbo. Have you picked up the northern tip of Little Abaco Island yet?" Paul asked.

"It's just coming into view off the starboard bow," Jim answered.

"Great," Paul said. "There's a nice little cove about 20 miles down the coast. We can spend the afternoon there. Later, we'll go into Marsh Harbor and take on some more fresh water.

"I thought we had plenty—but I wasn't counting on those 15-minute showers your brother and sister like to take! I'll have to talk to them about conservation."

Five hours later, the *Sea Mist* was again anchored in a small, protected cove. The Barclays all enjoyed more swimming and diving in the warm tropical water.

"This isn't a bad life," they all agreed. "It sure beats working and going to school!"

CHAPTER 5

Marsh Harbor

Paul had decided to stay anchored in the cove for the night. The next day they'd sail on to Marsh Harbor. *Sailing at night could be fun*, he thought, *but it sure made it hard to get enough sleep!*

As he lay in his bunk, Paul thought about what a great trip this had been so far. The kids were *super*. Ann was doing a first-rate job at raising them day by day. Before falling asleep, he made a mental note to tell her that.

The next morning they pulled up anchor and sailed down the coast to Marsh Harbor. Although it was only 40 miles away, it would take all day to get there. Heading into the wind, they would have to tack every hour or so.

At 6 o'clock that evening, the *Sea Mist* was tied up to a pier in Marsh Harbor. That night, the Barclays went to a little restaurant in town. It was the first restaurant food they'd had since leaving Miami.

Paul's plan was to leave Marsh Harbor early in the morning. This would be the longest leg of their trip. He wanted to visit Nassau—200 miles away.

After dinner, Paul and the kids headed back to their boat. Everyone was in great spirits as they walked along.

Then Paul suddenly stopped. "Let's call your mom and tell her how we're doing," he suggested.

"Great idea, Dad!" the kids cried out in one voice.

The call lasted more than 40 minutes as everyone took a turn talking. Paul ended the conversation. He assured Ann that everything was fine and that they'd be home in a week.

The next morning, the happy crew was bound for Nassau. It took a full day to round Great Abaco Island.

Now there was nothing but open sea between them and their destination. At

8 o'clock that night, Paul went into the pilothouse to check their position. He used *loran* to get the latest weather forecast. Jim was at the helm, and Aaron and Pam were playing a board game below deck.

Turning on the radio to marine weather, Paul started to adjust the dials on the loran set. He was startled by the radio report: *Severe low pressure is developing 100 miles south of Eleuthera. All mariners should avoid the area. High winds and heavy seas are forecast.*

The *Sea Mist* was heading in exactly that direction! Paul had to make some quick decisions. He'd been at sea in storms before, and it wasn't fun. And—if the storm got really bad—the danger could be deadly.

Paul decided to wait another hour. Perhaps the storm would change its course. If it veered toward the Florida coastline, they'd probably be able to avoid the worst of it.

An hour later, the radio reported a

hurricane watch. The storm was growing stronger. In fact, it was heading right for the *Sea Mist* at 15 miles per hour!

Paul was worried. He knew that he couldn't outrun the storm—but he had to try. He went up on deck and told Jim to change course 90 degrees starboard.

CHAPTER 6

The Storm

The seas had now built to five or six feet. Rain was starting to fall, and the wind had picked up.

A sudden flash of lightning lit up the darkening skies. Then sparks flew from the top of the radio antenna.

Oh, my gosh! Paul thought to himself. *Did that lightning hit our antenna?*

He ran into the pilothouse and looked in horror at the radio. Smoke was pouring out of it and a strong smell of burnt wiring was in the air! Even before he checked it out, he knew that the worst had happened: *The radio was gone because of a freak bolt of lightning!*

Aaron and Pam came up on deck. They had stopped playing their game because the pieces kept sliding off the board.

"What's happening, Daddy?" Pam asked. "Why is it getting so rough?"

"I'm afraid there's a storm coming," he answered. "If it doesn't change course, it will be much worse by morning. You guys better get into your rain gear and put on your life jackets. And no matter what happens—do *not* take them off!"

The tone of Paul's voice convinced the children that this was no time to argue or make jokes.

"Aaron, you and your sister go below. Tie down everything that might move around as the boat rocks. Jim, take the helm. Do your best to hold us on course while I secure everything on deck."

Paul tied lines around everything he could. But even simple jobs were difficult on the pitching boat. Water was now washing over the deck as the bow plowed into the eight-foot waves.

Paul worked his way back to the stern where Jim was fighting to hold the *Sea Mist* on course.

"Jimbo, I think we should take the sail down and run the motor now."

"Sure, Dad. I've just been thinking the same thing," Jim answered.

"Okay now, you hold course and I'll take her down."

Lowering the sail was no easy job in the howling wind and rain. Gathering and tying the sail to the boom took all of Paul's strength. But he eventually got it down and tied securely to the boom.

Darkness came—but tonight there would be no sleep for anyone on board the *Sea Mist*. The tossing and pitching of the boat made sleeping impossible. And Paul and Jim were both needed on deck to keep the boat from slamming sideways into the waves.

Paul had told Aaron and Pam to stay below deck. So much water was washing over the deck now that he was afraid one of them might be swept overboard.

At morning's light, the situation was no better. The storm was at its full height. Winds were up to 50 miles per hour, and the waves rose 15 to 20 feet. It was raining so hard it was hard to see anything.

Paul took the helm and told Jim to go below for a break. He'd been on deck all night, and he had to be bone tired! Paul sighed. He now wished that he'd never invited his children on this trip.

Just then a large wave drove the boat almost 10 degrees to the right. Paul struggled to bring the boat back on course. But the enormous force of the sea was working against him.

Now, with the *Sea Mist* pushed almost sideways by the storm, a second wave hit. Paul heard a loud, splintering *crack*. At first he thought it was thunder, but when he looked up, he gasped in horror.

The top 20 feet of the mast had broken off! The tall pole smashed onto the deck just 30 feet from where Paul stood!

Immediately, Jim was back on deck yelling, "Dad! Water is pouring into the cabins from a hole in the deck!"

"Take the wheel, Jim. I'll have a look."

Walking on the deck was now very

difficult. Holding onto anything he could, Paul struggled to work his way forward. One careless step could easily get him swept over the side!

As he got close to the fallen mast, Paul saw the problem. The heavy timber had ripped a five-foot hole in the deck. Every time the bow dipped into a wave, thousands of gallons of water were washing over the deck. Much of that water was pouring down the hole into the cabins below. And there was no way at all to repair the deck in these high seas!

Paul also knew that the saltwater would soon reach their motor. When that happened, they'd lose the ability to steer. Then he and the kids would be totally helpless. The pounding waves could kill them.

This is the last straw! Paul thought to himself. *The* Sea Mist *is going to sink. At most, we have 10 minutes.*

"We're going into the life raft," Paul shouted down to the kids. "Grab any provisions you can—and make it fast!"

Just as Paul untied the lines securing the life raft, Pam and Aaron scrambled up from below. Each had an armful of stuff.

All four Barclays tumbled aboard the raft as Paul cut the final line. Now they were free of the sinking sailboat.

"We're going to tie ourselves to safety lines," Paul shouted.

But as he spoke, another wave stood the little raft on its stern. Paul heard Pam yell, "*Daddy!*" But when he turned toward her, she was already gone!

CHAPTER 7

Girl Overboard

Jim watched in horror as his sister fell into the raging sea. Without hesitating, he dove in after her.

"No, Jim! Jim!" Paul shouted in desperation. But the sound of the storm drowned out his words.

Paul could see nothing. His son had disappeared! One moment the raft would be high on the crest of a large wave. A second later, it was deep in the trough with a wall of water on each side.

Then a miracle happened. For one split second, Paul could see Pam and Jim! Jim was holding onto his sister for dear life. With a couple of paddle strokes, Paul brought the raft alongside his children. Somehow he managed to pull them both aboard. Then he quickly secured safety lines to each of them.

He turned to his oldest son.

"Jim, that's the bravest thing I ever saw!" he said. "You saved your sister's life! I don't know how I can ever thank you."

Jim grinned. "Oh, I do, Dad," he replied. "When I get my driver's license, a little convertible might be nice. That is—if we ever get back on land!"

"We'll make it," Paul said grimly. "We'll see about the convertible later."

Paul looked around for their supplies. Almost everything they'd put on board had washed away! Now, all they had on the raft was packed in the survival kit.

It wasn't much. He made a quick mental list. They still had a 10-by-10-foot canvas tarp, a few tins of preserved food, and a pint of fresh water. They also had a fishhook with 40 feet of line, a flare gun with three flares, a waterproof case with a few matches, a small pocket knife, and a flashlight.

Paul knew how serious things were. They were miles from land and had very little food and water. But that wasn't the worst thing. Having no radio, they couldn't even send out a call for help.

Without an SOS call, no one would come looking for them—because no one even knew their sailboat had sunk!

Sheer exhaustion overwhelmed all four of the Barclays. Huddled together for warmth, they fell asleep—all except Aaron. He had an idea that he thought might save the day.

First, he slipped off his rubber rain pants and tied a tight knot at the bottom of each leg. Next, using one of the paddles as a support, he tied the pants in an upright position.

Finally, Aaron used the 10-by-10-foot tarp to create a large funnel. The pant legs began to fill up with rainwater. But it was a slow process. Aaron's arms ached from holding the tarp in place. Every few minutes he had to put the tarp down and rest.

When he finally had both pant legs filled, he tightened the drawstring at the waist. Then he sat back to rest. *Some water might spill out,* he thought to himself, *but most of it would be okay.*

When everyone awoke at dawn, Aaron spoke up. "Well, guys, I don't think we have to worry about drinking water."

"I don't know, son. I'm afraid we don't have very much," Paul said.

"Oh, yes, we do. I collected it all night. I'm sure I've got at least two gallons— maybe three!"

Jim was puzzled. "Huh? How did you do that?" he asked.

Then Aaron described what he had done. His father was amazed.

"What a great idea! You're a real genius, son," he exclaimed.

"I know," Aaron said with a little smile. "And, Dad—in five years or so, you can put me down for one of those convertibles, too!"

Paul felt a thrill of hope. He knew they could survive for days without food—but water was another story. He marveled at his kids' spirit. Every one of them was handling this terrible situation better than he could ever have imagined.

Then Pam piped up. "I'm not drinking any water that Aaron stored in his pants. That's *gross*!"

In spite of all their hardships, Paul and the boys couldn't help but laugh.

CHAPTER 8

Life Raft

The eye of the storm was now 40 or 50 miles beyond the raft. The rough seas were quieting down. And although it was still raining, it was more of a drizzle than a downpour.

The Barclays were all wet and cold and hungry. *This will be a miserable day,* Paul thought to himself. *But the sea lanes between the Florida coastline and the Bahamas are heavily traveled. Rescue shouldn't take long. Maybe—with any luck—someone will pick us up today.*

At midmorning, Paul opened a tin of dried food. He divided it four ways, and they each had a cup of fresh water.

At midday Jim shouted, "Look! Isn't that a plane?"

Everyone scanned the sky.

"It sure is," Paul cried out. "Hand me that flare gun, Jim!"

Paul fired the flare into the sky—but the plane didn't turn around.

"What's the matter with that dumb old pilot?" Pam grumbled. "Can't he see our flare?"

"Don't worry. Another plane or ship will come along," Paul said.

He was also disappointed that the plane hadn't seen them. But he didn't want to let his discouragement show.

Paul knew how important it was for everyone to think positively. He smiled at the kids, hoping to get their minds off their miserable situation.

"I'll bet you that I can guess any number you pick between 1 and 100 in less than 10 tries," he said.

The three Barclay kids looked at each other blankly. Then Jim realized what his dad was trying to do.

"You'd have to be very lucky to do that, Dad. I don't think you can," he said.

"I bet I can," Paul boasted. "All you have to do is answer my questions with a yes or no. Heck—I can probably guess your number in only six or seven tries."

"No way, Dad!" Aaron laughed.

"Okay," Paul said. "Put your heads together and pick a number."

They huddled together at one end of the raft and agreed on the number 26.

"Okay, Daddy," Pam said. "We have our number."

Paul grinned and asked his first question. "Is your number larger than 50?"

"No," they answered.

Then Paul asked, "Is your number larger than 25?"

"Yes!" they shouted.

Then Aaron figured out what his dad was doing. "No fair, Dad. You aren't picking numbers."

Paul's face looked innocent. "I didn't say *how* I was going to do it. All I said was that I could guess your number in six or seven tries. And all you had to do was answer yes or no."

The kids rolled their eyes as Paul went

on. "Okay, are you ready? Is your number larger than 37?"

When the answer came back "No," Paul knew that their number had to be between 25 and 37.

While the kids were griping about the fairness of his method, Paul asked his fourth question. "Okay, guys—is your number larger than 30?"

Jim sighed and said, "No."

Paul asked question five. "All right. Is your number larger than 27?"

Another disgusted "No" came from the far end of the raft.

"Well," Paul said, "your number's got to be either 25 or 26. Let's see—which number shall I pick with my sixth try? I think I'll go with 26."

"Ha!" Pam cried. "You think you're so smart! You should be ashamed of yourself for taking advantage of a bunch of kids!"

Paul was starting to have fun with this. Clearly, his little game was getting the kids' minds off their problems.

"Let's see," he said. "What did we bet?"

"You know we didn't bet anything," Aaron answered. "And even if we did, we wouldn't pay because you cheated."

"Now, *you* have to be fair, Aaron. I didn't cheat—I just outsmarted you," Paul said with a wink.

They floated in the raft for the rest of the day. That evening they shared another tin of dried food and another cup of water. That night, the Barclays huddled together at one end of the raft. For a bit of warmth, they covered themselves with the tarp. Again, weariness took over. Everyone was soon asleep.

CHAPTER 9

Shark Attack

By 10 o'clock the next morning, the seas were down to a normal two feet. The sun was shining brightly. They all had the same thought: It would have been a beautiful day to sail on the *Sea Mist*. Too bad she was at the bottom of the ocean.

The sun felt good. It was the first time in days that everyone was warm. But Paul knew that the sun could also become a problem. They had no hats, no sunglasses, no sun-blocking lotion. He and Jim rigged the tarp to provide some shade on most of the raft.

As they floated in the afternoon sun, Pam decided to try to catch a fish. She'd never really enjoyed fishing before, but she'd become very bored.

Pam got out the line and hook before she realized that she had no bait. After thinking for a minute, she pulled bits of yarn and thread from her clothes. Then she wrapped them around the fishhook.

That looks pretty good, Pam thought to herself. Then she dropped her homemade lure over the side and let out about 30 feet of line. The rest she tied around her wrist. For a while she waited for a bite, but nothing happened. Before long, she fell asleep.

Then a sharp tug on the line tied to her wrist woke Pam up with a start.

"I've got a bite!" she yelled out.

All eyes were on Pam as she began to pull in the fish line.

"Something pretty big is on here!" she cried out as she struggled with the line.

Moments later a 14-pound amberjack was flopping on the bottom of the raft!

Paul was excited. Of course, raw fish was far from his family's favorite food. But at least it would provide nourishment. He also knew that some people consider raw fish to be a real treat.

"Hey, that's good work, sis!" Jim said,

patting his little sister on the back.

Paul took out his pocket knife and began to clean the fish. The head, tail, and intestines he tossed in the water. As he was cutting the meat from the bones, Aaron shouted, *"Dad! Is that a shark?"*

Paul looked up. To his horror, the dorsal fin of a large shark was less than 20 yards away! It was slicing through the water, heading right for the raft. Attracted by the fish parts, the shark was looking for an easy meal.

Paul knew that if the shark struck, its sharp teeth would tear the raft apart.

"We've got to keep him away from the raft! Jim, grab the other paddle and help me fight him off."

For just a moment, the dorsal fin disappeared. But then it surfaced right alongside the raft. The raft tipped to one side as Paul and Jim jabbed at the shark with their paddles.

With a flap of its powerful tail, the shark swam 10 to 15 yards away. Then it turned and charged the raft again.

Pam was crying with fear. Aaron wasn't too far from doing the same. They'd both seen the movie, *Jaws*. Neither one of them had forgotten what happened to the fishing boat in that film.

Again and again the shark charged the rubber raft. Again and again Paul and Jim used the oars to strike out at it. But whenever they managed to drive it away, it always turned around and came back.

Finally, on one charge, the shark lifted its head out of the water when it was four feet away. Paul brought the edge of the paddle down with all his might. It caught the huge fish on the top of its nose. With a swipe of its powerful tail, it was gone.

"That *had* to hurt!" Jim said.

"I sure hope so," his father gasped. "Maybe this time he's gone for good."

The little group watched for hours, but the fin never reappeared. Finally, they relaxed enough to eat some of Pam's raw fish and drink a cup of water.

"Isn't it amazing what we'll eat when we're really hungry?" Aaron exclaimed. "I'd *never* eat this at home—but out here it tastes pretty good."

"It will keep our strength up—and that's the important thing," Jim said.

That night they heard the sound of an airplane engine. The kids yelled and waved as Paul fired the second flare into the sky. But the engine sound slowly faded as the plane flew on.

CHAPTER 10

A Ship

Paul was secretly losing hope as the sun came up the next morning. He'd been so *sure* they'd be rescued by now! He had to keep a positive attitude in front of the kids—but inside he was feeling desperate.

They hadn't seen a boat since the storm, and they were quickly running out of food and water. Only one flare was left. *Things couldn't be much worse,* Paul thought to himself.

Nobody was talking very much. The dispirited kids all seemed to be deep in their own thoughts.

Pam was thinking about her mother. She wondered if she'd ever see her again. And she thought about how nice it would be to sleep in her warm bed. Of one thing she was absolutely sure: If they ever got rescued, she'd never set foot on a boat for the rest of her life!

Aaron's mind was on his mom, too. *I wonder if she knows what's happening to us,* he thought to himself. *No, of course she doesn't know. We lost our radio and couldn't send an SOS.*

Jim's spirits were higher than his brother's and sister's. Somehow he was still sure they'd be rescued. Maybe it would happen today. If not today, then tomorrow for sure. Football practice would start in a few days. He had to be back home for that!

Paul's thoughts were also on his ex-wife, Ann. His job had been the reason for their divorce. He was usually away for half the year—sometimes more.

Ann wanted a normal marriage. She wanted a husband who came home at night, and Paul couldn't blame her.

But he loved the challenge of his work. He was so well-respected that when a big construction job came up, Paul Barclay was the first man to be called.

Paul also liked to travel. At age 43, he'd already worked on four continents. And then there was the money. He was very well-paid for his work.

Yet Paul had thought many times about giving it all up. He'd considered taking a teaching job at a local college. Ann had begged him to do that.

"The money's not all that important," she had insisted.

Perhaps she was right. He missed her and the children a lot. But right now, he had to get his kids out of the mess he'd gotten them into. After that, he promised himself to seriously consider teaching.

The rest of the day went by without any new problems. When it got dark, they all fell asleep again. Several hours later, Aaron awoke. As he sleepily stared off toward the horizon, he thought he saw something.

He strained his eyes to see through the darkness. Yes, he was sure now! He saw a dim red light in the distance.

What had his father told him? A red light at sea is the portside running light of another vessel. But whatever the light was, it seemed to be going past them! There was no time to waste. Aaron grabbed the flare gun and fired their last flare into the night sky.

CHAPTER 11

Rescued

The huge cruise liner was heading back to Miami. First Officer O'Malley was on the bridge. He'd just gotten a report from the portside lookout.

"Mr. O'Malley, I believe we spotted a flare off the port beam."

O'Malley scanned the horizon with his binoculars, but he couldn't be sure. *I'd better notify the captain*, he thought.

Captain Turner answered the phone in his stateroom.

"Sorry to wake you, Captain. This is O'Malley on the bridge. We have a report of a flare off the port beam."

"Did you see it?" the captain asked.

"No, sir—but the port lookout did."

"Well, we're a little ahead of schedule, so let's check it out. Bring the ship around, O'Malley. I'll join you on the bridge in just a minute."

"Yes, sir," O'Malley answered.

Aaron shook his father awake and told him what had happened. Paul's first thought was worry. Had Aaron wasted their last flare?

Paul stared in the direction Aaron had pointed. He saw both a green and red light! That could mean only one thing: The ship had turned around and was heading directly toward them.

They were finally getting a break! Now Paul had to make sure that the ship could see the little raft in the darkness. He doubted that the ship's radar would pick up such a small object.

He ordered Aaron to fetch the flashlight from the survival kit. Aaron handed it to his father, but when Paul switched it on, nothing happened. *Dead batteries*, he thought. *Oh, no! Why didn't I check them out before we left?*

Back aboard the liner, dozens of pairs of eyes were now scanning the darkness for another flare. They could see nothing.

Finally, Captain Turner sighed.

"I guess it was a false alarm. Let's get back on our course," he ordered.

Paul estimated that the ship was about two miles away. When the huge bow started to turn away, the green running light disappeared. Paul's mind was racing.

"What more can I do?" he cried out. "Please—*don't leave!*"

Then he remembered the matches. Paul tore off his shirt and tied it around one of the paddles. The shirt was bone-dry from baking in the sun for two days. *This has got to work*, Paul silently prayed.

Paul lit several matches before the shirt caught fire. When it was fully ablaze, he started to wave the paddle back and forth above his head.

"*Please, oh, please, look back!*" he begged aloud.

Moments later, the portside lookout came running into the pilot house. "There *is* something out there, Captain. Look!"

Captain Turner looked out, and this

time he saw Paul's burning shirt!

"Left full rudder," he ordered. "Slow to one-third speed. And Mr. O'Malley—put your searchlights on whatever that is out there."

To the Barclays, the huge ship looked like a mountain approaching the raft. Then they were blinded by the bright glare of the searchlights. Finally, a voice from the ship's loudspeaker called out, "Hold on! We're lowering a boat for you."

Tears poured down Paul's cheeks as he hugged his three children. He couldn't remember a time when he had ever been happier!

Ten minutes later, Captain Turner greeted the Barclays as they scrambled on board the cruise ship.

"How long have you been out there in that raft?" he asked.

"Four days—maybe five," Paul said. "I'm afraid we've sort of lost track of time."

Captain Turner was sympathetic.

"I know you must be hungry. What can

we get for you folks to eat?"

"*Pizza!*" Pam and Aaron cried out.

"Yeah," Jim chimed in. "A pizza would taste just great right now."

Paul would have preferred a big steak, but he said, "Pizza all around then. This family sticks together."

"It will take about half an hour to get the pizzas ready," the captain said. "In the meantime, let me call one of the stewards. He'll show you a cabin where you can get a hot shower. Then we'll try to find you some warm clothes."

"Thank you, Captain," Paul answered.

Paul turned the shower water on as hot as he could stand it. It was pure pleasure. It had been five days since he'd bathed. The warmth on his skin felt great!

As the caked-on salt washed away, he thought of Ann. How would he explain all of this to her? How would she react? What a job that was going to be!

The steward rounded up some clothes for each of them. The fit wasn't perfect, but no one cared. The clean clothes were dry, warm, and soft—and most important— free of salt.

Captain Turner joined the Barclays as they ate their pizzas. Paul told him about the storm, losing the radio, and the sinking of the *Sea Mist*.

"Whew!" Captain Turner said. "You folks have sure had your share of bad luck! But things will improve now."

The soft beds and clean sheets felt like true luxury. The four refugees of the sea slept like babies.

CHAPTER 12

Back in Miami

The big liner docked in Miami at 8 o'clock the next morning. At the end of a long cruise, a ship is always a beehive of activity. It was no different today.

Some 1,200 passengers were leaving the ship. Most of them were bound for the airport to catch flights back to their hometowns. Luggage and duffel bags were stacked up everywhere.

But no one was stirring in the cabins where the Barclays slept. Finally, at 10 o'clock, Captain Turner ordered one of the stewards to go in and wake them.

He'd made arrangements for a car to take Paul and the children to a local hotel. As the family prepared to leave the ship, Captain Turner visited the cabin to say goodbye. One by one, each of the Barclays thanked him for their rescue and for all of his kindness.

"When we get some new clothes, we'll be sure to send these things back to you," Paul offered.

"Oh, don't bother, Paul. Why don't you keep the clothes as souvenirs of your adventure?"

After the two men shook hands warmly, the Barclays walked down the gangway to a waiting car.

Paul asked the driver to take them to the nearest mall so they could buy some clothes. He still had his wallet with a few hundred dollars and some credit cards.

Since the Barclays needed just about everything, the shopping trip took hours. It was late afternoon when they checked into the Miami Hilton with their new wardrobes.

The date was July 26. When he'd planned the trip, Paul had figured on returning to Miami on the 27th. Amazingly, they were back one day early!

Before doing anything else, Paul knew he had to call Ann. But how could he explain the last six days? Of course, she'd be happy that everyone was safe. But she'd also want to strangle him for putting their children in such danger!

All three kids noticed their dad's nervousness. Earlier in the day Aaron had said, "Don't worry about calling Mom, Dad. She'll understand."

Perhaps the wisest approach, Paul thought uneasily, would be to put Pam on the phone first. But what a big mistake that turned out to be!

Ann was at home. She answered the phone on the third ring.

"Hi, Mommy!" Pam cried out.

"Hi, darling! Are you back in Miami?"

"Yes, we got here this morning. You'll never guess what happened to us."

"What?" Ann asked.

"We hit a big storm with giant waves."

"*What?*"

"And the mast broke in half and made a great big hole in the deck!"

Ann gasped. She could hardly believe

what Pam was saying to her!

"Put your father on, please," she said.

"—And water came in the hole and the boat sunk."

"*What?*" Ann sputtered.

"—And I fell out of the life raft and almost drowned!"

"Honey, I need to talk to your father— *now!*" Ann said pleadingly.

"—Then a huge shark attacked our raft over and over again."

"Pam, put your father on this phone!"

"—And Daddy had to light his shirt on fire to get the ship to rescue us."

"Listen to me, Pam. Put your father on the phone right now. *And that's an order!*"

Pam handed the phone to her father. "Mommy seems mad about something. She wants to talk to you, Dad."

Paul reluctantly took the phone from his daughter. *This is going to be worse than everything we've just been through*, he thought to himself.

COMPREHENSION QUESTIONS

Recalling Details

1. In what month did the Barclays take their sailing trip?

2. What nickname had Pam been given by her father?

3. What item did Paul order all the kids to wear on deck?

4. What caused the *Sea Mist*'s radio to go out?

5. What natural disaster wrecked the *Sea Mist*?

6. What new job was Paul Barclay considering?

7. What did Paul burn to catch the cruise liner's attention?

Who and Where?

1. What group of islands did the Barclays visit?

2. At what city airport did the Barclay kids meet their dad?

3. Who was the first of the Barclay kids to steer the boat?

4. When the Barclays left Great Abaco Island, where were they headed next?

5. Who dived into the ocean to rescue Pam?

6. Who hit the shark's nose with a paddle?

7. Who first sighted the Barclays' life raft?